Rudolph The Red-Nosed Reindeer

By Eileen Daly

Illustrated by Milli Jancar

A GOLDEN BOOK • NEW YORK

Western Publishing Company, Inc., Racine, Wisconsin 53404

Once upon a time a young reindeer named Rudolph lived at the North Pole. Rudolph should have been a happy reindeer, but instead he was sad.

All the other reindeer had small brown noses. Rudolph's nose was big and red.

The other reindeer laughed at Rudolph and called him names. "Ha-ha! Look at Red Nose!" they said.

When the other reindeer played
snow slide, they never asked Rudolph
to play with them.

Poor Rudolph couldn't even play hide-and-seek with the rabbits. His nose made such a bright light that they found him right away.

Then one Christmas Eve something happened.
Santa was ready to choose his team to pull his sleigh.

The reindeer were very excited. Each one hoped Santa would choose him.

Rudolph wanted to go, too, but he was ashamed to have Santa see his bright red nose.

He hid in a toy box that Santa's elves had made.
No one would ever find him there!

Outside, the other reindeer lined up.

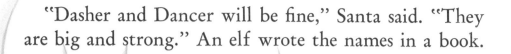

"Dasher and Dancer will be fine," Santa said. "They are big and strong." An elf wrote the names in a book.

"And I want Prancer and Vixen," said Santa, "and Comet and Cupid and Donder and Blitzen. They will be my team."

Santa gave the rest of the reindeer important jobs, too. One tried out toy trains. Another played with little Christmas kittens.

Inside the toy box, Rudolph heard the elves packing Santa's sleigh. "I don't care if they do laugh at me," he thought to himself. "I want to help, too."

The night was very dark. The elves bumped into each other as they put the harnesses and bells on Santa's team of reindeer.

It was so dark that Santa could not see his long
list of names.

Suddenly a soft red light lit up Santa's list. "Ho-ho!" boomed Santa. "I can see now! Who brought this red lantern?"

"It's not a lantern," said Rudolph, just a little frightened. "The light comes from my nose."

"Rudolph the Red-Nosed Reindeer!" said Santa.
"You will be the leader. Your bright, shiny nose will
show us the way!"

Rudolph held his head high. The other reindeer
helped put on his harness and bells.

Soon Santa and his reindeer were flying over roof-
tops. And proudly leading them all was Rudolph the
Red-Nosed Reindeer!